my many emotions

Disgust

Cherry Lake Press

Published in the United States of America by Cherry Lake Publishing Group
Ann Arbor, Michigan
www.cherrylakepublishing.com

Reading Adviser: Beth Walker Gambro, MS, Ed., Reading Consultant, Yorkville, IL
Content Adviser: Emily Fragapane, M.Ed., Ed.S., Nationally Certified School Psychologist, RYT200
Book Designer: Jennifer Wahi
Illustrator: Jeff Bane

Photo Credits: © Phatplus/Shutterstock.com, 5; © Regreto/Shutterstock.com, 7; © Lapina/Shutterstock.com, 9; © Photographee.eu/Shutterstock.com, 11; © Aleksandra Suzi/Shutterstock.com, 13; © Jihan Nafiaa Zahri/Shutterstock.com, 15; © Dmytro Zinkevych/Shutterstock.com, 17; © AlexandrMusuc/Shutterstock.com, 19; © fizkes/Shutterstock.com, 21; © Oksana Kuzmina/Shutterstock.com, 23; Cover, 2-3, 6, 12, 22, 24, Jeff Bane

Cherry Lake Press is an imprint of Cherry Lake Publishing Group.

Library of Congress Cataloging-in-Publication Data

Names: Devera, Czeena, author. | Bane, Jeff, 1957- illustrator.
Title: Disgust / by Czeena Devera ; illustrated by Jeff Bane.
Description: Ann Arbro, Michigan : Cherry Lake Publishing, [2021] | Series: My many emotions | Includes index. | Audience: Grades K-1
Identifiers: LCCN 2021004908 (print) | LCCN 2021004909 (ebook) | ISBN 9781534186965 (hardcover) | ISBN 9781534188365 (paperback) | ISBN 9781534189768 (pdf) | ISBN 9781534191167 (ebook)
Subjects: LCSH: Aversion--Juvenile literature. | Emotional intelligence--Juvenile literature. | Social learning--Juvenile literature.
Classification: LCC BF575.A886 D48 2021 (print) | LCC BF575.A886 (ebook) | DDC 152.4--dc23
LC record available at https://lccn.loc.gov/2021004908
LC ebook record available at https://lccn.loc.gov/2021004909

Printed in the United States of America
Corporate Graphics

table of contents

About the author: Czeena Devera grew up in the red-hot heat of Arizona surrounded by books. Her childhood bedroom had built-in bookshelves that were always full. She now lives in Michigan with an even bigger library of books.

About the illustrator: Jeff Bane and his two business partners own a studio along the American River in Folsom, California, home of the 1849 Gold Rush. When Jeff's not sketching or illustrating for clients, he's either swimming or kayaking in the river to relax.

Sometimes, you might feel **Disgust**.

Yuck!

How would you describe Disgust?

Disgust can be strong and **intense**
It can cause a quick **reaction**.

Disgust can come with strong smells. Like your grandma's new perfume. Or someone's lunch at school.

Sometimes, Disgust comes when you try a new food. You might not be used to the taste. The **texture** might be different.

How does Disgust feel to you?

Disgust can make your stomach **churn**. You might feel sick.

These are all normal reactions. Disgust is meant to keep you safe from things that can hurt you.

However, Disgust can be harmful. It can hurt someone else's feelings.

Slow down. Think about how you want to react. Will plugging your nose hurt your grandma's feelings? Will spitting out your food upset the person who made it?

You can't control when you feel Disgust. But you can control how you react to it. Try drinking a glass of water. Think before you speak.

How do you
show Disgust?

Remember, it's okay to feel Disgust. New things might make us **uncomfortable**. But that shouldn't stop us from trying new things.

glossary & index

glossary

churn (CHURN) experience a strong or uncomfortable feeling

disgust (diss-GUHST) a strong feeling of dislike or annoyance for something considered sickening or bad

intense (in-TENSS) felt deeply

reaction (ree-AK-shuhn) a behavior or response to something

texture (TEKS-chur) the feel and appearance of something

uncomfortable (uhn-KUHM-fur-tuh-buhl) uneasy

index